Weekly Reader Children's Book Club presents

Stone Soup

Retold by William Furstenberg • Illustrated by Hans Wilhelm

Weekly Reader Books
Middletown, Connecticut

This book is a presentation of
Weekly Reader Children's Book Club.
Weekly Reader Children's Book Club
offers book clubs for children from
preschool through junior high school.

For further information write to:
Weekly Reader Children's Book Club
1250 Fairwood Ave.
Columbus, Ohio 43216

"Look!" said Winston as he scrambled to the top of the hill. "I can see a little village, way down there in the valley."

"I see it, too!" cried Clara happily. "It looks like such a friendly place, doesn't it?"

"I certainly hope it is," said Winston. "We've been on the road for three days now without a meal."

"And three nights sleeping on the hard, cold ground," sighed Clara. "I'd give just about anything for a soft bed to sleep on tonight."

Winston put his arm around his sister. "Don't worry, Clara," he said. "I'm sure we'll find something to eat in the village. And you'll have your soft bed, too. People all over the world are kind to travelers like us."

Winston and Clara were still a long way from the village. But the townspeople already had seen them coming. Now, these people were rich enough. And they had plenty to eat. The trouble was, they hated strangers. And they were just as mean and stingy as could be.

"See those two strangers headed our way?" said one. "Why, they'll eat everything in town, if we let them."

"You're right," said another. "And they mustn't find out how rich we are, either. Or surely they'll want us to share with them."

So everyone in the village got busy hiding food and money. The town butcher closed his shop. He snatched the roasts and chops and steaks out of his store window. Then he hid them down in the cellar. The butcher shop looked bare as a bone.

The town banker locked up his bank. He shuttered the windows and put a sign on the door: "Bank Closed. All Out of Money."

The village innkeeper hid every key to every room. No guests were staying at the inn. But, no matter, he hung a sign over the desk anyway: "Inn Full. Next Inn Ten Miles."

The farmer's wife ran out to the garden. Quickly, she picked every cabbage, carrot, and onion. Then she hid them under her bed.

The townspeople put chickens and sausages in their closets. They stuffed rice and potatoes into drawers and cupboards. They even lowered buckets of milk down into their wells. It wasn't long before every single scrap of food was out of sight.

Now the villagers could go about the day as usual. But even the richest of them wore the poorest, oldest clothes. Each man put a sad, hungry look on his face. And each woman clutched at her stomach as if she hadn't eaten in days.

Our travelers reached the village gates with high hopes. "Look at all the fine, big houses," said Winston. "It looks like a lot of rich folks live here."

"Mmmm," said Clara. "I think I smell a fresh-baked apple pie."

"Me, too," said Winston. "And my apple-pie-smelling nose is pointing to that big, white house over there."

Winston and Clara went right up to that house and knocked on the door. It opened just a crack.

"What do you strangers want?" said a harsh voice from behind the door.

"Please," said Winston. "My sister and I have come a long, long way. We've had nothing to eat for three whole days, and . . ."

"Go away!" said the voice. "We barely have enough food for ourselves." The door slammed shut with a bang.

Clara went up to a man who was crossing the street.

"Please, sir," she said politely. "My brother and I are a long way from home. We could use a hot meal. And a place to sleep."

"That's not my problem," said the man gruffly. "There's no room at the inn. And as for food, well, we had a bad harvest. There's almost no food left in the whole town."

Then the man put the hungriest possible look on his face. He grabbed his stomach with both hands. "I'm hungry, too," he said as he went on his way.

Winston and Clara knocked on every village door.
They stopped everyone who passed by. "No food!"
"No room!" "We're as poor as you are!" "Go away!"
The answer was always the same.

"Whatever will we do now?" said Clara, as they
slumped down on a bench in the village square.

"I don't know," said Winston sadly. "I feel sorry for
these people if they're as badly off as they say."

"I feel a lot sorrier for them," said Clara, "if they've
been lying to us. They must have hearts of stone."

"Hey!" shouted Winston. "That gives me an idea!
Come on, Clara, follow me!"

"What for?" asked Clara. "Where are we going?"

"Just follow me. I'll explain it along the way," said
Winston.

Then Winston told Clara his idea. And they knew
just what they had to do.

Winston and Clara ran to the bell in the village square. They tugged hard on the rope, and the bell rang and rang. Right away, the whole town came running.

"What's the meaning of this?" asked the mayor. He shoved his way to the head of the crowd. "We only ring the town bell for emergencies."

"Sir," said Winston. "This *is* an emergency. We've knocked on every door. We've talked to everyone who would listen. I'm sure you'd like to help us, if only you could. So it must be true, then. You're as poor and hungry as we are."

"So," said Clara, "now's the perfect time to make stone soup!"

"Soup?" said the mayor. "From stones?" He threw back his head and laughed heartily. The crowd began to laugh, too. Stone soup, indeed!

"Go home, everybody," said the mayor. "These youngsters are not only poor and hungry. They're crazy, too! Whoever heard of such a thing as stone soup?"

"But wait!" said Winston, tugging at the mayor's coat. "Have you ever heard of the great Wadoo of Wixiland?"

Now, there is no such thing as a Wadoo. And there's never been a place called Wixiland. But, the mayor thought to himself: *Wixiland? Wadoo? These sound like important things a mayor should know about.*

"Everyone who knows anything knows about the great Widda, er, Wadoo," snapped the mayor. "So what?"

"Well, sir," Winston went on, " as you well know, the great Wadoo of Wixiland is the wisest Wadoo of all. My father was his best student. So he rewarded my father with his secret recipe for stone soup. My father passed the secret on to me. You see, when you know how to make stone soup, you can never go hungry."

Hmmm, the mayor thought to himself. *Maybe there's something to this stone soup after all. Think how rich we could be if we could make soup from stones. Our little village would be famous.*

"Give us a chance," Clara pleaded. "All we need from you is a soup kettle. What's the harm in that?"

"All right, then," said the mayor at last. "Bring them a soup kettle. And make it a big one. Let's see if these two can feed the whole town with stones."

So three of the strongest townsfolk brought out the largest soup pot in the village. Winston and Clara grabbed two buckets and ran to a nearby stream. It took many, many bucketfuls to fill the pot with water.

Next they gathered up firewood. They built a huge bonfire under the kettle. In no time at all, the water was boiling and bubbling merrily.

Winston picked out four large, round stones lying in the village square. "How lucky you are!" said Winston. "You have just the right kind of stones in your village for stone soup."

Clara carefully wiped the dirt from each stone. Then she dropped them, one by one, into the kettle with a splash.

Winston and Clara sat down to wait. But it wasn't long before the crowd grew restless.

"What's happened to that magic soup you promised us?" cried one of the villagers.

"You can't hurry good stone soup," Clara replied. "Stones are very hard. It takes a lot of cooking to make them tender and juicy."

More time passed. At last, Winston went to the steaming pot and dipped in his spoon. He blew on the soup to cool it. A hush fell over the crowd.

"Ahhh," said Winston as he tasted the broth. "Stone soup is so tasty, even when it's plain, like this."

"Let *me* have some," said the mayor eagerly.

"Oh, not yet, sir," said Winston. "It needs salt and pepper first."

Right away, the mayor sent his wife home for salt and pepper. In just a few minutes, she was back—bringing some fresh herbs, too. Clara sprinkled salt, pepper, and herbs into the bubbling kettle.

"You know," said Winston as he stirred the soup, "stone soup is so much better when it has a few carrots in it. Or maybe a cabbage or two."

"Winston!" said Clara with a frown. "You know that these people are as poor and hungry as we are. What would they be doing with carrots and cabbages? I'm sure if they had some, they'd tell us."

"I have carrots and cabbages under my bed!" said the farmer's wife, not thinking what she was saying.

"Your bed?" said Winston with a look of surprise.

"I mean, er, the *cabbage bed*," she quickly explained. "Maybe I can even find a carrot or two. It can't hurt to go see."

So off the farmer's wife ran to her bedroom. And in just a few minutes, she was back. She brought a sack full of carrots, cabbages, and onions, too.

Winston and Clara chopped up the vegetables and threw them into the pot.

"Winston?" said Clara as she stirred the soup. "Doesn't our stone soup look just a bit thin? It could use a little milk, don't you think?"

"Milk?" said Winston. "Clara, milk is for rich people. Where in the world would these poor folks get milk?"

"From our wells!" said the butcher's wife without thinking.

"Wells?" said Clara with a look of surprise.

"I meant to say, ah, I might *well* find a drop or two left," she explained. "It won't hurt to go see."

Off the butcher's wife went running. She soon returned, hauling two huge buckets brimming with fresh milk. Winston and Clara poured the milk into the pot.

Winston stirred and stirred the soup. "You know, Clara," he said. "Stone soup is just not quite the same without potatoes."

"Winston!" Clara scolded. "I know that even very poor people have potatoes to eat. But we've been to every house in this unhappy village. And we didn't see a single potato anywhere."

"The potatoes are in drawers and cupboards!" said the banker's wife.

"In drawers and cupboards?" said Winston with surprise.

"Oh, what I mean is, maybe some potatoes *rolled behind my cupboard*," she explained. "Or maybe one or two *fell into a drawer*. It can't hurt to go look."

So off the banker's wife ran to her cupboards and drawers. Quick as a wink, she was back with a basket full of potatoes. Winston and Clara peeled them, cut them up, and tossed them into the pot.

"You know," said Clara, speaking loudly enough for the whole village to hear. "My father often had dinner with the emperor of BongoBongo."

The townspeople looked blankly at each other. Not one had ever heard of BongoBongo. But it must be a very important place to have a real emperor in charge.

"This emperor," Clara went on, "served stone soup just like ours. Only his *always* had meat in it."

"Just imagine!" the townspeople said to each other. "A little meat would make our stone soup good enough for an emperor!"

"But, Clara," said Winston sternly, "you know this is not BongoBongo. And these people certainly are not emperors. How can you even talk to them about meat? You saw the butcher shop. Bare as a bone!"

"All the meat is in the cellar!" the butcher said.

"In the cellar?" said Clara with surprise.

"Oh, I mean, I'm the *seller*," explained the butcher quickly. "But, maybe there are some scraps left I didn't sell. No harm in looking."

Off ran the butcher to the cellar of his shop. And in no time at all, he was back with both arms wrapped around a huge chunk of beef. Winston and Clara cut it up and threw it in the pot.

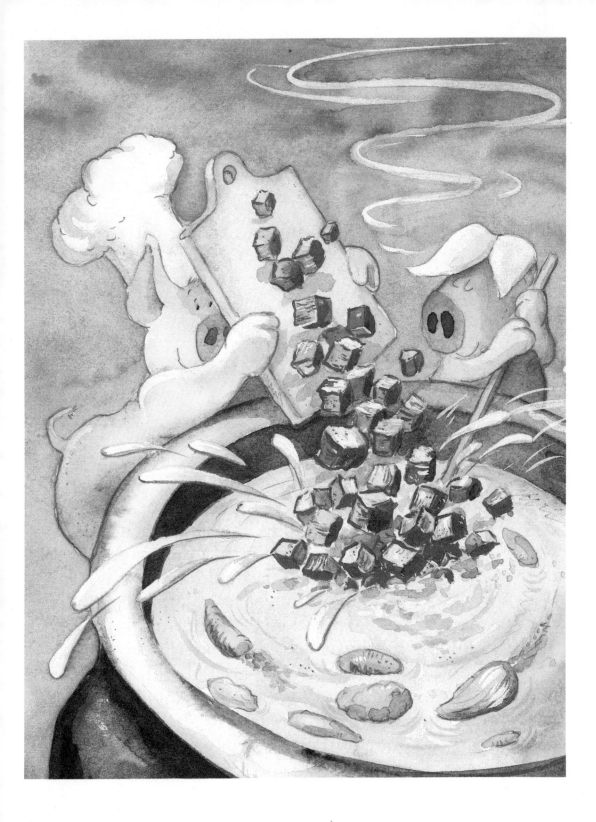

The wonderful smell from the soup kettle was making the whole town hungry. Especially the mayor.

"I can't wait another minute!" he said. Then he snatched up a spoon and dipped it into the soup. As he tasted it, the crowd was quiet as could be.

"Why," said the mayor with delight, "this is truly the most wonderful soup I've ever tasted. And imagine! There's nothing in it but stones and water!"

The whole town cheered and shouted with joy. They hoisted Winston and Clara high on their shoulders. How proud they were of this magical pair! So why not have a feast in honor of the two cooks who made soup from stones?

Chairs and tables were set out in the square. Roast chickens and sausages came out of hiding. There was fresh cider to drink. And all sorts of cakes and pies for dessert.

The townspeople ate and drank long into the night. When the last drop of stone soup was gone, the innkeeper took Winston and Clara to the inn. He gave them his best room. Quickly they fell asleep in soft beds at last.

Next morning, everyone in the village turned out to see Winston and Clara on their way.

"You've taught us some wonderful magic," said the mayor. "How can we ever thank you?"

"By serving stone soup to all hungry travelers," was Winston and Clara's reply.

And to this day, the little village is known the world over for its big heart. There is always food and rest for a tired and hungry traveler. And it's all because of Winston and Clara. They gave the village a recipe for stone soup. And a recipe for kindness, too!